Eight Wild Nights

A Family Hanukkah Tale

Brian P. Cleary

Illustrated by
David Udovic

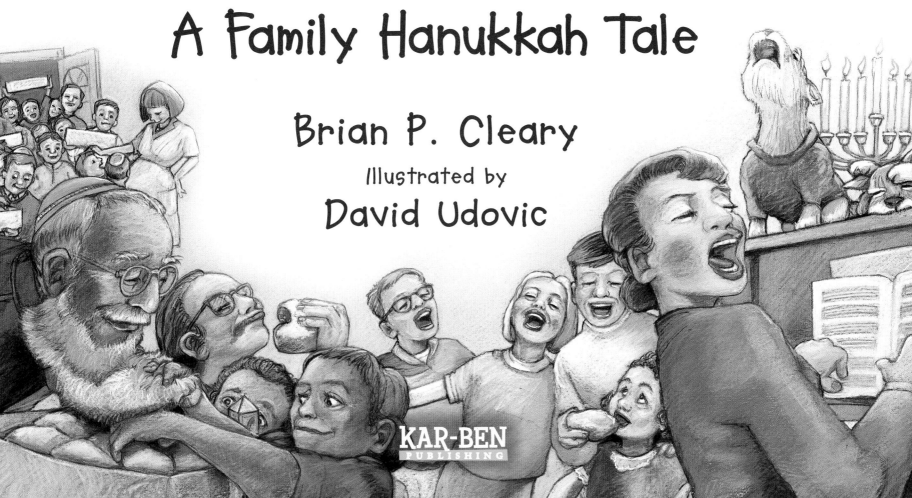

KAR-BEN
PUBLISHING

For Grace, Ellen and Emma —B.P.C.

To my parents —D.U.

Kar-Ben Publishing, Inc.
A division of Lerner Publishing Group, Inc.
241 First Avenue North
Minneapolis, MN 55401 U.S.A.
1-800-4KARBEN

Website address: www.karben.com

Library of Congress Cataloging-in-Publication Data

Cleary, Brian P., 1959–
    Eight wild nights : a family Hanukkah tale/ by Brian Cleary ; illustrated by David Udovic.
        p.   cm.
    Summary: A large family celebrates Hanukkah by cleaning the house, entertaining guests, and
    preparing delicious food.
    ISBN-13: 978-1-58013-152-0 (lib. bdg. : alk. paper)
    ISBN-10: 1-58013-152-2 (lib. bdg. : alk. paper)
    (1. Hanukkah – Fiction. 2. Stories in rhyme.) I. Title: 8 wild nights. II. Udovic, David,
    1950– ill. III. Title.
    PZ8.3.C555Eig 2006
    (E)—dc22

Manufactured in the United States of America
3 4 5 6 7 8 – DP – 12 11 10 09 08 07

About Hanukkah

Hanukkah is an eight-day Festival of Lights that celebrates the victory of the Maccabees over the mighty armies of the Syrian King Antiochus. When the Maccabees came to restore the Holy Temple in Jerusalem, they found one jug of pure oil, enough to keep the menorah burning for just one day. But a miracle happened and the oil burned for eight days. On each night of the holiday, we add an additional candle to the menorah, exchange gifts, play dreidel, and eat fried latkes and sufganiyot (jelly donuts) to remember the victory for religious freedom.

This time of year always,
The bedrooms and hallways
Get vacuumed, and
straightened and dusted.
The kitchen is spotless,
No light bulb is watt-less
And nothing that's showing
is busted.

Each frying pan's shining,
As plates in the dining
room gleam, we await the arrival
Of eight days of guests,
Friends and family, and pests,
Who will threaten our very survival.

I look at the driveway,
And as they arrive, they
resemble a herd that's stampeding,
We're outnumbered highly,
but, clever and wily,
And ready to start with the greeting.

Our neighbor, Miss Fetter
Brings her dog in a sweater ––
A shaggy mess stuffed in angora!

He drools and he sheds, On the sofas and beds
And nearly knocks down the menorah.

He chases poor Ira, our cat, past Aunt Myra

Who spills all the applesauce topping . . .
"The latkes, I deem,
will be served with ice cream,"
My mom says
while wiping and mopping.

Although Grandpa Dave
Has been told to behave,
He's still quite a
prank-loving joker.

He'll hide the new dreidel
'neath the couch or the cradle
and teach us kids
blackjack and poker.

He'll tell the whole table
His Hanukkah fable,
"When I was a boy," he will say,
"our bathroom was low
on the T.P., you know,
Enough for just maybe one day.

"My dad told me,
'Sonny, we won't have the money
For a week and a day to buy more,'
But that small roll it lasted
After eight days had passed it
Could paper the whole corridor."

My cousin who's six
Has learned a few tricks.
He gathers up all of the gelt!
And hides it down far
In an old VCR
And waits for the chocolate to melt.

His sister who's three
Likes to take things from me,
Like the book I just got from Aunt Donna.
If I shoosh her or shoo her,
This kid, turning bluer,
Will cry until next Rosh Hashanah!

Aunt Helen makes blintzes, And everyone winces
When she brings her serving plate by.

So like Maccabaeus
Who fought hard to free us,
We bravely will give it a try.

What present for me
Is beside the TV?
A gameboy?
A laptop computer?

Instead it's pajamas
That look like my grandma's
Which Mom says just couldn't
be cuter!

Great Uncle Morris,
And his new wife, Delores
Brought 17 of my step-cousins

And donuts galore
From the kosher food store,
With jelly and glazed by the dozens.

And even though she
is a little off key,
Aunt Rachel will lead us in song.
And while we're rejoicing,
As each girl and boy sing,
It's a way-out-of-tune
sing-a-long!

Sis always handles the lighting of candles,
And each year forgets the right order.
But by the eighth night,
They're all lit, left to right,
With wax drippings big as a quarter.

After eight days of eating,
Of loud noise and greeting,
A great miracle's happened here:
We're quiet and calm,
and all getting along,
and we can't wait to do it next year!